Mail Order B
The Holiday Bride

By
Faith Johnson

Clean and Wholesome Western
Historical Romance

Table of Contents

Unsolicited Testimonials

By **Glaidene Ramsey**
★★★★★ I so enjoy reading Faith Johnson's stories. This Bride and groom met as she arrived in town. They were married and then the story begins.!!!! Enjoy

By **Voracious Reader**
★★★★★ "Great story of love and of faith. The hardships we may have to go through and how with faith, and God's help we can get through them" -

By **Glaidene's reads**
★★★★★ "Faith Johnson is a five star writer. I have read a majority of her books. I enjoyed the story and hope you will too!!!!!"

By **Kirk Statler**
★★★★★ I liked the book. A different twist because she wasn't in contract with anyone when she went. She went. God provided for her needs. God blessed her above and beyond.

By **Amazon Customer**
★★★★★ Great clean and easy reading, a lot of fun for you to know ignores words this is crazy so I'll not reviewing again. Let me tell it and go

By **Kindle Customer**
★★★★★ Wonderful story. You have such a way of showing people that opposite do attack. Both in words and action. I am glad that I found your books.

FREE GIFT

Just to say thanks for checking our works we like to gift you

Our Exclusive Never Before Released Books

100% FREE!

Please GO TO

`http://cleanromancepublishing.com/gift`

And get your FREE gift

Thanks for being such a wonderful client.

Chapter One

Cloud Springs, New Mexico, 1895

Clara Whittaker sat down gingerly on the hard wooden bench at the small train station, trying to spread the skirt of her gown around her so that her ankles weren't exposed. She blinked owlishly as she gazed around, taking in the scene through the thick fog of steam from the train. She had to pinch herself that it was real—that she really was sitting on a rickety bench in New Mexico, waiting to be picked up to begin a whole new life. It was a long, long way from her cossetted life back in Boston.

How did this happen? How did I get here?

The few people who had disembarked with her at Cloud Springs rushed around, dragging battered trunks from the train. There were smiles and kisses and sometimes shrieks of delight as people greeted each other after a long journey. She watched as trunks were hoisted atop wagons before the people climbed aboard, heading off to their homes, or so she assumed.

A stab of pure terror filled her heart as she gazed around. She had never felt more alone in her entire life…and as the platform cleared, she realized that she really *was* alone now. Apart from the grey-bearded station master, that is, who belched slightly as he sat down in his small booth before burying his face in a newspaper.

Where is my ride? Have they forgotten about me? Oh, dear Lord, what am I going to do?

Clara fought back tears as she stood up, walking to the edge of the station. She had been a foolish woman indeed. She had traveled thousands of miles from Boston to this small backwater in New Mexico to become the wife of a man she had never met before. She had found the small advertisement in the *Matrimonial Times* only two months ago. It had been brief. A man called Jebediah Huxley, who claimed he ran a successful ranch in New Mexico, wanted a wife. And Clara, in her desperation to escape her impossible situation, had responded.

The reply had been swift. She had sent the best photograph of herself, taken at one of the finest photography studios in Boston only months before. Jebediah Huxley had written back, saying he was pleased and wanted her to journey out west to join him in his life. And Clara had written back, accepting the offer.

And that was how she was here, alone and terrified and seemingly abandoned in this Godforsaken place.

Clara blinked rapidly, staring at the town beyond the train station. Cloud Springs. She had thought it an endearing, pretty name for a town…but her eyes showed her that the town's reality was far, far different from its name's promise. Cloud Springs was the smallest town she had ever seen, not that she had seen many towns, not having left Boston that much at all. Uncle Eustace, who had reared her from an infant, hadn't been fond of taking her on day trips. Or anywhere, for that matter. Uncle Eustace had lived for his work as one of the city's finest barristers, and she had barely seen him at all.

Clara bit her lip so hard it almost bled. Cloud Springs seemed to have just one long, dusty main street and a few scraggly houses clustering around it. She saw a general store, a saloon, a church, and a haberdashery. Her eyes drifted along the road. There was a blacksmith as well. But that was it. It was so far removed from the bustling metropolis of Boston that Clara felt like she may as well have journeyed to the moon.

Her heart hit the ground with a thump. Her uncle, who was her only relative in the world, was dead. She had left the only home she had ever known, which had been sold a month ago and was awaiting possession by its new owners. She had never been more alone and vulnerable in her life. And to add insult to injury, it was early December, with only a few weeks until Christmas.

How did I come to this? Oh, Lord, what have I done?

Clara felt beads of sweat trickling down her neck. She was so exhausted after the long journey that she could barely stand up, and it was *hot*. The sky was the brightest blue she had ever seen, and she was surrounded by desert – strange red and gold rock formations, spindly cactus-like vegetation, and other outlandish-looking plants. It contrasted sharply with her hometown, which had been two inches deep in snow when she had left. It was like she had stepped inside a bizarre dream…or was it a nightmare?

"Ma'am? Are you Miss Whittaker?"

Clara spun around, her heart beating as fast as a jackrabbit. She had been so absorbed in her contemplation of this frightening place that she hadn't even heard footsteps approaching her. A tall man was standing before her with a slightly amused expression.

Clara gasped. The man wore a faded blue shirt, dirty trousers, and long black boots, with a frayed kerchief knotted around his neck. A crumpled, wide-brimmed hat sat atop his head, stained with sweat. Clara noticed that soft dark curls brushed against the collar of his shirt. Her eyes flickered to his face. He had bushy dark eyebrows, dark stubble on his granite-like jaw, and a bushy dark moustache. Eyes the color of moss looked at her beneath slightly hooded lids.

He must be a groom or another Huxley family servant, thought Clara, taking in his disheveled, shabby appearance. *He is dressed in the garb of a laborer of some sort.*

Clara took a deep breath, raising her chin. She had been dealing with servants her entire life, and there was a certain way to address them. Uncle Eustace had always drummed that into her.

"Yes, I am Miss Whittaker," she said in the most polished voice she could muster, fighting her exhaustion and dismay. "You work for the Huxley family? If you could just direct me to the carriage before you take my trunk?" She pointed to her luggage, containing all she possessed in the world now. It was a sobering thought. She felt another stab of terror and desolation.

The man's moss-green eyes darkened to almost black. His granite jaw tightened. Clara's eyes widened, waiting for his response. She wasn't used to being kept waiting by servants. Uncle Eustace had run a tight ship, and most of his servants tiptoed around the house, fearful of his growl. But he had always been more bark than bite. He had been a terribly busy man, that was all, and didn't suffer fools gladly. And that was just the way of it in their tight, Boston circle.

To Clara's consternation, the man standing in front of her gazed at her insolently, those alarming eyes flickering over her from head to toe. She almost felt like he had reached out and slapped her.

"The *carriage* awaits you at the front of the train station, *Miss Whittaker*," he said eventually, emphasizing every syllable of her surname as if it were an insult.

Before she could respond, he turned his back on her, almost stomping to the trunk.

Well, that takes the sweet cake, thought Clara, her heart thumping hard. *Not only have I journeyed to the most dismal town on this earth, but the servants here are as rude.*

Clara bit her lip hard again. The insolent servant hoisted up her trunk as easily as a bag of peanuts. The man must have muscles made of iron, for she had struggled mightily with that trunk the entire journey, and it had taken two railwaymen to drag it from the train on her behalf.

He didn't wait for her. He simply hauled it up and stomped out of the train station. Clara scurried after him.

She stopped abruptly, gaping at the vehicle in front of her. She realized now why his voice had been dripping with irony when he had referred to it as a carriage. This was a rickety wagon with a single workhorse attached to it, the white canopy flapping desolately in the wind.

The man hauled the trunk into the back of the wagon before climbing aboard, taking the reins, staring stonily ahead. Clara realized he wasn't even going to help her climb aloft. Taking a deep breath, she scrambled aboard, scraping her left shin.

Clara turned her head away from him. She just couldn't look at him, fearing those treacherous tears would rise again and spill over. And she wasn't going to give an impudent servant the satisfaction of seeing them.

"Giddup," he commanded in a gruff voice, flicking the reins.

The wagon slowly started moving down the main road of the town. Clara's vision was blurry as she stared at the general store, the saloon, and the little weatherboard church.

There aren't even any Christmas decorations, she thought mournfully, thinking longingly about the center of Boston, awash with showy decorations for the season and vendors hawking ornaments and cards. *Not even a few strings of lights.*

At the edge of the town, near the blacksmith, they turned left, traversing a narrow dirt road.

They rode in strained silence, not saying a word, heading further away from the small town into the desert beyond. But Clara was no longer seeing anything. She started this journey with such hope. But now, she was very fearful of what Mr. Jebediah

Huxley, her husband-to-be, was going to be like. And how was she going to endure living in this dusty backwater, with rude servants, amid such appalling poverty?

Had she just made the biggest mistake of her life?

Chapter Two

Jeb Huxley tightened his grip on the reins as he glanced covertly at the stiff-backed woman sitting next to him on the wagon. Her face was turned away from him, gazing out at the landscape whizzing past. All he could see was the back of her bonnet, from where a few wispy tendrils of auburn hair escaped, flying in the wind.

Jeb's jaw hardened. The woman had thought he was a servant—and he had never been spoken to so curtly in his life. He frowned slightly. She was beautiful and refined, with a round face, skin like white marble, and large doe-like blue eyes. Clearly, she wasn't working class. But then, she hadn't been brought here to scrub floors or milk cows, had she?

Jeb mulled over the puzzle in his mind. His mother had suddenly, and quite bizarrely, decided she wanted a 'companion'—a woman from the East, no less. A woman with refinement and breeding, who could sit with her doing needlepoint and press flowers into books and other such nonsense that Jeb neither had the time nor the will to understand.

His frown deepened. The puzzle of it intensified. His mother wasn't that sort of refined lady at all. Hannah Huxley was still the working matriarch of Cordillera, their ranch that had been in the Huxley family for two generations. She still split wood, rounded cattle, and birthed calves if she needed to, although that wasn't often anymore. Still, she was a whirlwind, always busy with practical matters around the ranch. His mother didn't live an idle life. He had never seen her press a flower into a book in his life, and she had never expressed a desire to, until she had suddenly sent for the young woman sitting so rigidly beside him.

Maybe Ma is finally getting old, he thought, his heart flipping. *She'll be turning sixty in a few months. Perhaps that's what this is all about.*

Jeb gave a painful sigh. This trip into town to pick up his mother's new companion had turned into a trial. The woman was undoubtedly as refined as his mother hoped, but impossibly rude and uppity. Jeb had never met anyone from the East before, and he had certainly never met someone who considered themselves a real *lady*. And despite her obvious beauty and class, Jeb didn't like anyone who put on airs and graces, thinking they were better than everyone around them.

Maybe I should tell her who I am, he thought, anger rising in his breast again as he thought about the rude way she had spoken to him on the train platform. *Maybe I should tell her she's working for me, not the other way around. I'm the one who will be paying her wage, after all.*

Jeb was so lost in his reverie about the uppity woman sitting beside him, who he was about to be forced to live with, that he almost missed the turn to the ranch. He only managed to pull up Silky, the horse, at the last minute. The back wheels of the wagon almost became airborne as they rounded the corner. He had to suppress a smile of satisfaction when he heard Miss Whittaker give a yelp of alarm.

It didn't take long to traverse the narrow track to Cordillera. The ranch loomed before them. The sun had just begun to set behind it, spreading pink and orange streaks across the sky. Jeb felt a wave of weariness wash over him. All he wanted now was to wash, eat, and then fall into his favorite rocking chair on the porch to stare at the sky before an early night. It had been a long, hard day. But then, the life of a head rancher was always hard.

"Here we are," he barked to the woman, jumping down. "You go on in while I get your trunk. The kitchen is around back. That's where they will all be."

The uppity Miss Whittaker pursed her lips in disapproval, clearly thinking he was speaking to her a tad bossily for a servant. But he was too tired and out of sorts to tell her the truth just yet. She would find out in the fullness of time. He suppressed another smile at the anticipation of seeing the shock on her face when she realized he *was* the boss here as he headed to the back of the wagon to get her trunk. He didn't think Miss Whittaker would like it one little bit.

***

Clara hesitated, gazing from the ranch to the rude servant and back again. He had told her to head around back, but she wasn't sure. Shouldn't there be a welcoming committee on the front porch to greet her after her long journey? After all, she had traveled so far to get here, and she was about to become the mistress of the ranch.

The ranch. *Cordillera*. Mr. Jebediah Huxley had told her the name of it in one of his letters.

She stared at the homestead. It was large, with a wraparound veranda, but it wasn't made of brick or sandstone like the imposing mansions in Boston. This house was constructed from roughhewn timber. There were several outbuildings as well, spreading haphazardly around it. She heard the low bellowing of cattle in the distance and a mournful howl in response.

Clara felt a shiver of fear. She hoped it was a domestic dog making the sound rather than a coyote.

Clara took a deep breath as she studied the ranch, still expecting the front door to burst open and her welcoming committee to emerge. But when it didn't happen after another minute, she shook herself, walking around the back of the house as the servant had instructed her to.

There was light around the back, and she heard loud chatter as well as bursts of laughter emanating from inside. Clara hesitated, overwhelmed with fear. She was a shy person by nature and had never socialized much at all to learn the skill of it. Uncle Eustace had home-schooled her and had never been big on community functions or gatherings. It had been an isolated life.

And now she was thousands of miles away from the safety of her home and about to walk in on a group of strangers. Once again, she felt like she was in the midst of a bizarre dream. Surely, she would wake up at any moment?

Hesitantly, she knocked on the back door. Immediately, it flew open. A girl of around eight years old with golden hair in sausage curls gazed at her curiously.

"Who are you?" she squeaked, staring at Clara as if she were an apparition rather than a flesh and blood person.

Clara's jaw dropped. But before she could form a reply, the girl was surrounded by people gawking at Clara. Her eyes flew from one to the other, taking them in. There were two small boys, around four and five. She also saw a heavily pregnant, dark-haired young woman with sparkling green eyes and an older woman with the same eyes, filled with warmth and amusement.

"Well, look at what we have here," cried the older woman, grabbing Clara by the arm and pulling her inside. "You got here at last! We've been waiting for you! Supper is about to spoil…"

Clara's head whipped around, taking it all in. She was standing in a large kitchen with a wood stove in one corner and a wide fireplace. In the center of the room was a long wooden bench laden with upended flour, sugar, and other food. The smell of meat casserole suddenly drifted towards her. Clara's stomach growled. It had been a long time since she last ate.

Everyone pressed around her, staring at her avidly. Clara tried to take a step back. It was overwhelming. And it was so *hot* in here.

"Yer pretty," piped up one of the small boys. He turned to the younger woman, tugging on her skirts. "She's pretty, Ma!"

At that moment, the rude servant walked into the kitchen. He didn't look at Clara or the gaggle of people surrounding her. Instead, he sat down on a chair near the fire, peeling off his long black boots before tossing them carelessly to the side.

Clara's eyes widened in shock. It was not the action of a servant. It was the action of a man who ruled the hearth.

Her stomach dropped in fear and confusion. Who exactly *was* the dark-haired, insolent man?

Chapter Three

Clara's mind was still reeling, staring at the dark-haired man. She knew her mouth had dropped open, and she was staring in a rather stupid manner. But before she could say anything, the older woman steered her away from the others.

"You sure look shocked, Miss Whittaker," declared the woman, smiling broadly. "I guess it's been a long trip!" She drew a deep breath. "My name is Hannah Huxley. Welcome to Cordillera."

Clara smiled timidly, studying the woman. She had dark hair streaked with silver, coiled into a tight bun, and a brown-lined face, as if she spent a lot of time beneath the sun. She was dressed in a plain white blouse and a long brown skirt.

"This is my daughter, Lillian," continued the woman, pointing at the younger woman. "She and my grandchildren are staying with us while her husband, Roy, is working interstate." Her smile widened. "And the young'uns are Pearl, Jimmy, and Robbie."

"How do you do?" squeaked Clara, her mind moving fast. The older woman had said her surname was Huxley. Clearly, she was a relative of Clara's husband-to-be. His mother?

Her eyes were drawn back to the dark-haired man sitting by the fire. Another stab of uncertainty and fear speared her heart.

"And where is my husband-to-be?" she asked in a timid voice.

There was a sudden silence, followed by a burst of laughter from both Hannah Huxley and her daughter. After a moment, the children joined in.

And then, Clara realized both women were gazing at the dark-haired man in a quite pointed manner.

"Oh, dear Lord," stammered Clara, her head starting to spin. Could it be…? But then, why hadn't he said anything at the train station?

But before she could grapple with that thought, the dark-haired man suddenly stood up, his face thunderous.

"Ma," he said in a deceptively calm voice. "What does she mean asking where her *husband to be* is?"

Clara's jaw dropped again, almost hitting the floor. She was so shocked she felt like she had just been hit in the stomach as she realized the truth of the situation.

The dark-haired man was clearly the son of Hannah Huxley, not a servant. She was reasonably certain now he was Jebediah Huxley, her intended. And it was further evident that the man himself had no idea of that fact. Until now.

What was going on?

"Now, Jeb," said Hannah Huxley in an equally calm voice. "I only did it this way because I knew you would bellyache about it.

It was better to get the girl here so you could see what a fine woman she is. She sent us a photograph, so we knew she was a real beauty." She smiled proudly at Clara. "And she's prettier in the flesh, if that is possible!"

Jeb Huxley's face turned puce. *"What?"*

His mother's smile widened. "You work too hard, Jeb. You need a *wife*, my boy. You're nearing thirty, and it's time you settled down." She took a deep breath. "You always tell me you will start courting one day, but it never happens. You're in danger of turning into an ornery old man, Jeb…"

The man cussed loudly. Clara felt herself pale. She had never heard such language in her life.

"I don't need a wife!" he cried, his face luminous with anger. "And you need to stop interfering in my life, Ma."

He glared at her and Clara before grabbing his boots and pulling them on. His face was still tight with anger as he strode out of the kitchen by the back door, slamming it behind him.

Clara couldn't help it. She burst into tears.

Immediately, she was surrounded by people. Hannah Huxley's arms were around her, hugging her tightly. Lillian started clucking in a soothing way. Even the children pressed against her, patting her awkwardly.

Clara had never been in a communal embrace before. She had never been embraced at all, really. Uncle Eustace had certainly never done so. Her uncle had kept her at arm's length and was a cold, emotionally distant man. And the servants who had brought her up weren't affectionate with her, probably out of fear that they would do the wrong thing. And they were paid to look after her, after all.

It was pleasant. It was actually, surprisingly, very pleasant indeed.

But then, the reality of her situation hit her again. As lovely and comforting as these people seemed to be, it appeared that they had duped her. Hannah or Lillian or both of them must have written to her, pretending to be Jebediah Huxley, brokering the marriage on his behalf without his knowledge.

Her husband-to-be didn't want to marry her. He hadn't even known she was coming here as his intended. And judging by the violence of his reaction when realizing the truth of this appalling situation, he certainly wouldn't be marrying her at all.

She was thousands of miles from her home. A home that was no longer there, anyway. She had hardly any money to start over again. And to add insult to injury, it was almost Christmas.

What on earth was she going to do?

***

The following day, Clara hesitated at the entrance to the kitchen, gazing around. Surprisingly, despite the turmoil of her mind, she had passed out entirely in the narrow bed Hannah Huxley had led her to the previous night, sleeping as soundly as a log. She guessed it must have been the exhaustion of the trip.

The smell of boiling coffee and frying bacon, eggs, and grits filled the air. Lillian, a crisp white apron wound around her swollen belly, was at the wood stove, tending the food. Hannah was setting the table. There was no sign of the children, but Clara could hear high-pitched squeals outside.

There was no sign of Jebediah Huxley, either.

Hannah glanced up from her task, seeing her. "There you are, Clara! Come and sit down. You must be hungry. You barely ate a mouthful last night."

Clara swallowed hard, nodding, before stepping into the room and taking a chair at the long table. Suddenly, she noticed the Christmas tree perched in a far corner of the room. Somehow, in the dramatic events of the previous evening, she hadn't seen it at all.

It was a pine tree, just like the Christmas trees back home, if a bit spindlier. But whereas the trees that Uncle Eustace always bought were massive, taking pride of place in the drawing room and decorated in expensive, store-bought glass ornaments and elaborate candles, this tree was far smaller. There were no store-bought ornaments, either. Instead, the tree was decorated with strings of ribbon and yarn, threaded with popcorn and dried fruit. There were a few battered tin ornaments, as well.

Clara's heart lurched. It was simple but beautiful and heartfelt. She just knew that the children playing so happily outside had decorated this tree under the watchful eyes of their mother and grandmother. In contrast, she had never been allowed to go near or touch the Christmas trees at home. Uncle Eustace had been adamant about that. He had heard too many stories about people catching fire from the candles. And besides, he was always too busy at work to make time to decorate a tree with his orphaned niece. The servants always did it, and Clara would simply watch, longing to join in.

Somehow, as she gazed at this tree, the thought of that was the saddest thing.

She was jolted out of her reverie about Christmases past by Hannah, placing a hot tin mug of coffee in her hand. Clara smiled timidly at the woman, accepting the cup. It was time to clear this mess up and figure out what she was going to do now.

"Mrs. Huxley…"

"Hannah, if you please," interjected the woman, smiling at her warmly. "We don't stand on ceremony in these parts, Clara."

"Hannah," said Clara, taking a sip of coffee before placing the mug down. It was strong and good. "Where is…Mr. Huxley this morning?"

"Jeb left the house hours ago," said Hannah, sitting beside her, sipping her coffee. "He starts work as soon as the sun rises and doesn't stop until sundown. It's a hard life, running a ranch." She hesitated, reaching out to take Clara's hand. "Don't worry, girlie. He will come around to the idea of you in his own good time. Now, do you want to come with me into town today to do some errands? We should keep you busy to take your mind off my ornery son."

Clara smiled slowly. The woman was so warm and friendly that somehow she forgave her for duping her into this. Hannah Huxley just wanted a wife for her only son. That was all, even if her action had been misplaced and doomed to failure.

And Clara needed to get back into the town. She needed to get to the train station to find out when the next train back east would be leaving and make sure she was on it. Hannah didn't need to know that her plan was going awry and would never bear fruit. Not yet, at any rate.

Even if there was nothing in Boston for her to go back to, either.

Clara took a deep breath. "Yes, I would like to go into town with you, Hannah. Thank you."

Chapter Four

Clara gazed around the small house in Cloud Springs, her eyes flickering to the timber ceiling, which had so many gaps in it that sunlight was beaming down upon her. This was the third house in Cloud Springs she and Hannah had visited today, and it was in the worst condition. She had never dreamt that people could live in such poverty.

She shuffled her feet uncomfortably, not knowing what to do. She couldn't sit down at the small rickety table as Mrs. Vickers, the woman who lived here, and Hannah were sitting on the only chairs in the place. Hannah was smiling at Mrs. Vickers over the top of her large wicker basket, which was laden with coffee, flour, butter, eggs, and a small ham. A Christmas gift that Hannah had told her she and her family performed every Christmas season for the poor in the local community.

"They often have nothing, the poor dears," Hannah had told her on the ride into town. "And even less at Christmas. It means they can celebrate the holy day along with the rest of us."

Clara had tried to suppress her surprise. Uncle Eustace had never performed acts of Christmas charity in the community. It would never have occurred to him to do so. As far as her uncle was concerned, the poor deserved everything they got. He had often waxed lyrical at the supper table, stabbing his fork in the air as he lectured Clara about the feckless poor, telling her that they were a lazy, idle bunch who were almost always beholden to the demon drink.

But Mrs. Vickers didn't seem drunk, or idle, or feckless. Instead, she just looked exhausted. Still, the woman had been welcoming, smiling widely when she opened the door to them, ushering them inside.

Hannah was clearly well-known in the town and well-liked.

As Hannah and Mrs. Vickers chatted, Clara kept gazing around. Despite the obvious poverty, the house was as neat as a pin. There were even a few scraggly flowers in a jam jar in the middle of the table.

The woman takes pride in her home, thought Clara. *She is doing her best with very little.*

Clara took a step back, colliding with a large wooden crate on the floor.

A plaintive wail emerged from within its depths. Clara almost screamed in shock. Was it an animal?

But as she leaned over, blinking in the darkness, she saw a tiny fist waving in the air and the outline of a small face beneath a hand-knitted bonnet. Her heart shifted. It wasn't an animal. It was a baby who was looking at her intently before it broke out into a huge, gummy smile.

"Oh," cried Clara. "I did not realize you had a baby, Mrs. Vickers. I did not mean to disturb…"

The woman laughed, getting up and picking up the baby from the crate, patting its back in a circular motion. "It is quite alright, Miss Whittaker," said the woman, smiling broadly. "This is our May. She is needing a bottle soon anyway. Would you like to hold her?"

Clara hesitated. She had never held a baby in her life. What if she dropped it?

"Go on," urged Hannah, smiling as well. "You need the practice, Clara. For when you have your own babies one day."

Clara blushed to the roots of her hair. Gingerly, she accepted the baby. May reached out a hand, managing to grab a stray tendril of Clara's hair and yanking it mightily.

"Ouch," said Clara, smiling at the baby. "You have a good grip, young lady."

They all laughed. Clara gave the baby back to her mother, feeling strangely elated, if still unsettled.

May is just a baby, she thought, her heart shifting again. *And yet, she does not even have a proper crib. She must sleep in a crate.*

She watched as Mrs. Vickers prepared the baby's bottle, settling down to feed May at the table. The young mother looked at her infant with such love and pride as she fed her that Clara had to blink back tears.

***

The day flew by, going from house to house, delivering the Christmas gift baskets. Clara found, to her surprise, that she was actually enjoying meeting the townsfolk of Cloud Springs. They were all welcoming and friendly and so grateful for Hannah's kindness. Clara had never felt more involved or valuable in her life. She was used to idling her days away doing pointless needlework or flower arrangements or other frivolous activities that Uncle Eustace had deemed suitable for a proper lady.

She was so engrossed that she realized she hadn't even managed to slip away to get to the train station. They stepped out of a house and saw the wagon waiting to take them back to the ranch. Jebediah Huxley himself was sitting at the front of the wagon, reins in hand. His face was as hard as granite.

Clara blanched. It was the first time she had seen him since the previous evening when he had stormed out of the kitchen. It was so very awkward.

But Hannah didn't seem to think so. She waved cheerily at her son.

"You are early," she called, walking quickly to the wagon. Clara trailed behind her. "I still have two houses to attend."

The man rolled his eyes. "You told me three o'clock. So here I am."

Hannah frowned slightly. "Why don't you take Clara back to the ranch, and I will finish here? She must be tired and needing a rest. I will get a lift back with old Mr. Davidson. He will be heading our way in an hour or so."

Jebediah Huxley didn't look pleased at the suggestion. Clara blushed. But Hannah was pushing her onto the wagon, and she didn't know how to refuse. The next minute, they were away, with Hannah waving merrily, a big grin on her face. Clara was sure she had planned the whole thing.

They journeyed in awkward silence until they reached the track leading them to Cordillera. Clara glanced at the man sitting next to her. How could she break this impasse between them?

"I am sorry," she said in a halting voice. "So very sorry. I did not know that this was a ruse to get me here. I sincerely thought that it was you writing to me and that you wanted a wife."

He didn't answer for a moment. Clara's heart sank. She didn't want him to be her enemy, even if he would never become her husband.

"I know it isn't your fault, Miss Whittaker," he replied eventually, a sour note in his voice. "It was my mother entirely. But I am tired of her interfering in my life. You seem a fine woman. But I do not want a wife."

Clara's heart sank again. This was all such a mess! And the worst of it was she was actually starting to feel sorrier for Jebediah Huxley than for herself now.

Yes, he had been rude to her yesterday…but that was only because she had been arrogant and dismissive with him first, thinking he was a servant. Her face burnt with shame at the thought of it, especially after her day getting to know the townsfolk of Cloud Springs and realizing they were just people with the same thoughts and feelings as her. And if they were just people, then servants were, as well.

I was taught to treat people badly, she thought, her heart lurching. *I knew no better. But my old life is gone forever. And I can choose to be whomever I want now.*

"I am sorry," she repeated, tears springing to her eyes. "I am sorry for the way I spoke to you yesterday. I am sorry that you have been put into this position." She took a deep, ragged breath. "I am sorry for everything."

He didn't reply for a moment. Clara fought back the tears. It seemed he was determined to think the worst of her forever. And she didn't blame him one little bit.

Chapter Five

Jeb glanced at the stricken face of the auburn-haired woman sitting next to him in the wagon. Miss Whittaker seemed close to tears. He was still angry and annoyed by the whole thing, but he felt pity rear up—an unexpected emotion.

And her eyes looked impossibly blue shimmering with tears. Almost as blue as the sky above them.

How pretty she is, he thought suddenly. *Ma wasn't lying about that.*

She was apologizing. There was not a trace of her arrogance from yesterday. And this mess really wasn't her fault. She had responded in good faith to an advertisement requesting a wife, thinking he had initiated it. She had uprooted her whole life to journey here.

"Why did you do it?" he asked in a quiet voice. "Why did you come here?"

She looked surprised. "I didn't have much choice," she replied slowly. "My uncle, who reared me, died suddenly. I thought he might leave me a small inheritance – enough to live on – but it seems he was actually in great debt. I received nothing from his will." She paused. "My only other choice was to find someone to marry in Boston. You see, I am entirely without skills, Mr. Huxley. How can I support myself?"

Jeb felt another flash of pity. She was very refined, but that was a liability in this world when alone and vulnerable.

"Jeb," he said suddenly. "Call me Jeb. Everyone else does."

Her face twisted slightly. "Then you should call me Clara, as well."

Jeb smiled. "Clara. It is a pretty name for a pretty lady."

She blushed, ducking her head. Jeb cleared his throat, feeling uncomfortable. Yes, she was *very* pretty, but for all intents and purposes, she was as useless as a porcelain doll. A person had to be tough and capable to survive out here. And Miss Clara Whittaker was more fragile than a hothouse flower and just as likely to wilt under pressure.

His mother, as confident as she was that she had done the right thing in sending for this woman, had made the wrong choice. A refined lady from the East could never become the next matriarch of Cordillera. Not that he was looking for the next matriarch, of course. Not at all.

"And why are you so set against marriage, Jeb?" she asked, as if reading his mind.

Jeb's face twisted. How could he answer her honestly? How could he tell her that he had made a vow to himself not to marry until he had turned Cordillera into the most successful ranch in New Mexico? How could he tell her he was driven to do it and couldn't afford any distractions, least of all a wife and children? How could he tell her that he had silently made the vow as he watched his father dying, trapped beneath a fallen windmill when Jeb hadn't called out to him to move in time?

He couldn't tell her any of that at all. It was something he didn't like to think about, for it stirred up too many old, painful memories.

"I just don't," he said in a hard voice.

They rode the rest of the way in silence again. Jeb felt a flash of guilt at her stricken face, then a flash of irritation that he was forced into this position to even feel guilty about her. The sooner Miss Clara Whittaker left Cordillera and the entire territory, the better.

***

The next day, Hannah declared that she was heading into town for more Christmas duties, asking Clara if she would like to accompany her again. Clara accepted with alacrity, painfully aware that she must get to the train station as soon as possible to book a ticket back to Boston. Especially after her stalled conversation with Jeb Huxley in the wagon yesterday.

He is quite adamant he doesn't want a wife, she thought. *I am not wanted here. His mother and sister cannot change that fact, no matter how hard they try.*

In town, they headed to a tiny hall at the back of the church. Clara was surprised to find it was a hive of activity, with people everywhere. Children were running around, weaving in between the adults. Some people were standing on the stage with pieces of paper in their hands. She spotted what looked like a small manger with a tiny doll nestled amongst straw.

She turned to Hannah. The older woman had refused to tell her what exactly they were doing today, saying all would be revealed. "What is happening here?"

Hannah smiled broadly. "Why, it is the annual Christmas pageant, of course!" She studied Clara's face intently. "Have you never been involved in one, my girl?"

Clara shook her head mutely. She had heard of Christmas pageants but had never even seen one, never mind participated. Uncle Eustace had always scoffed at the notion of them, calling them amateur theatrics and a waste of time.

At that moment, Hannah was called away. Clara wandered the hall a bit aimlessly, watching everyone, until Hannah caught up with her again, taking her arm firmly.

"You can help Mrs. Lyall with the angels' wings," she said, steering her to a corner of the hall. "She needs all the help she can get. I take it you know how to sew, Clara?"

Clara nodded. "Yes," she whispered. "I can do needlepoint…"

"That's good enough," said Hannah, introducing her to Mrs. Lyall before rushing away.

Within minutes, Clara was engrossed in the work, chatting to Mrs. Lyall and two other women who came to help. They were all very friendly and welcoming. The hours flew by happily. But when the reverend called a break, Clara managed to slip out, seizing her chance. The train station was only a short walk away.

The same grey-whiskered station master was in the ticket booth, reading the newspaper. He set it down reluctantly to serve her. To Clara's dismay, he told her that the next train east was on the day after Christmas, which was still a whole two weeks away. But she had little choice but to accept it, spending almost all of her last remaining coin on the trip back home.

As Clara walked back to the hall, tucking the train ticket into her sleeve, she gazed around at the little town. It had seemed so dismal and decrepit when she had first arrived here. But even now, it was as if she were seeing it through different eyes. And as she heard the cheerful chatter from the church hall, alive with the spirit of Christmas, her heart shifted slightly in her breast.

Strangely, she was going to miss this place. Just a little. But she knew she didn't belong here. The problem was, Clara had no idea of where she belonged at all anymore.

***

That night at Cordillera, after supper, Clara walked onto the front porch, leaning against the railing. Her breath caught in her throat as she gazed up at the night sky. She had never seen a sky like it. It was as if a million stars were hovering above her head, sparkling like crystal, strewn randomly across it as if they had been flung like sand onto paper.

The night sky isn't this glorious in Boston, she thought dreamily. *There really is something special about this place. Something mystical.*

There was a slight cough behind her. Clara spun around, her heart racing. She could just make out a figure sitting in a rocking chair, obscured by darkness.

"Magnificent, isn't it?" said a deep male voice. "I could watch it for hours."

Clara's heartbeat intensified. It was Jeb Huxley. She watched, spellbound, as he slowly got up, coming to lean on the railing next to her.

Clara held her breath. She didn't know why, but his proximity disturbed her in some way. He was just so tall and handsome, with his dark good looks and muscles hardened by work. His ·hooded eyes, as green as moss, held an amused glint as they beheld her. She couldn't fathom now why she had ever believed he was a servant. Jeb Huxley exuded masculine authority.

"I…I didn't mean to disturb you," she stammered.

He stared at her for such a long time that Clara started to fidget.

"You are disturbing me," he replied eventually, a slight edge to his voice. "But not in the way you believe, Clara." He reached out, touching her face ever so slightly, like the flutter of a butterfly's wing. "Your skin is so milky white. Have you ever spent any time in the sun in your life?"

Clara blushed fiercely. "Not much at all. And when I have, I always wear a bonnet and carry a parasol."

He grinned. But it was fleeting. The next second, he stepped back, turning his face to the night sky. Clara felt a stab of unreasonable disappointment. Something had just passed between them, pulsating as strongly as one of those impossible stars in the sky. But she had no idea what it was.

Chapter Six

Jeb gripped the porch railing tightly, trying not to look at her again. He had been falling into those big blue eyes of hers as if he were drowning, and that wasn't good. It wasn't good at all. He should say goodnight to her and leave right now.

But he didn't. He found he didn't want to leave her yet. It was just polite to get to know her a bit, wasn't it, before she left Cordillera? Because there was no way she was staying on. His mother might believe he would eventually succumb to Clara's womanly charms, but he knew better. He knew the reason why he couldn't take a wife yet, and there was no way his mother or sister or *anyone* was going to change that fact.

He was safe. And he was her host. It would be rude not to chat with her just a little.

"Do you like it here?" he asked softly, glancing at her sideways. "It must be very different to a big city like Boston."

"Totally different," she said, laughing a little. "It is like chalk and cheese." She hesitated. "But to answer your question – yes, I like it here very much. It has grown on me."

He nodded approvingly, pointing into the distance. "Do you see that mountain range?"

She squinted. "Just. It is shrouded in darkness. But I have seen it often during the day. It is beautiful."

"It is," he agreed. "This ranch was named in its honor. You see, the word *Cordillera* means mountain range in Spanish. My great-grandpappy saw the range and said he wanted to live in its shadow for the rest of his days. And so he built this ranch and did just that."

She turned to him. "So your family has been here for quite a while, then?"

Jeb nodded. "We have. My great-grandpappy was a fur trader from the mid-west. He traveled the Santa Fe trail to trade his furs and liked it here so much he decided to stay." He paused. "Ranching is in our blood, now. I couldn't imagine living anywhere else."

"It is hard being away from your home," she said, her voice catching in her throat. "This is the first time I have ever been away from mine."

"What is it like in Boston?"

Clara smiled wryly. "Boston is a big city, as you say. You would be alarmed by all the noise and people. One of the things I notice most about here is the silence that surrounds you." She hesitated. "But I must say it is disconcerting that there is no snow here for Christmas time. It almost always snows in Boston on Christmas Day. It seems… wrong, somehow."

She looked wistful and sad. He had to restrain himself from reaching out to comfort her.

"We live close to the mountains," he said in a ragged voice. "Sometimes, it *does* snow at Christmas here. But not that often." He hesitated. "I'm sorry you miss your home. And I'm sorrier than I can say that my mother dragged you all the way here for no reason, Clara."

She flinched slightly, and her face crumpled. Jeb felt a small stab of guilt and shame. But he had to be honest with her, didn't he? He couldn't give her false hope. That would be even crueler than making her journey west for nothing. He couldn't take a wife yet. And that was that.

Clara took a deep breath, squaring her shoulders, looking him straight in the eye. "I should go inside. Good night, Jeb."

He nodded, feeling awkward and awful. She walked past him, brushing against him on her way inside. Jeb jumped. It felt like an electric current had just passed through him.

He gaped after her, feeling shaken to the core. What was wrong with him?

***

Two days later, Clara left the house, heading off on a walk. She had told Hannah and Lillian that she wanted to find something special to place on the Christmas tree. But really, it was just an excuse to spend some time by herself and explore more of this strange but alluring country before she left New Mexico forever.

"Stay close to the house," Hannah had warned, giving her a basket. "Don't venture too far, Clara. You don't know the terrain, and it's easy to get lost."

Clara had agreed not to wander too far. But as she walked, she found herself so mesmerized by the exotic vegetation and desert landscape that she kept going just a little bit further, feeling as if she were sinking into a dream.

The sky is so blue here, she thought in wonder. *And the landscape is so dry and barren. Red and gold sand abounds as far as the eye can see. The contrast is simply stunning.*

She stopped walking abruptly, taking a deep breath, taking it all in. She felt like she was imprinting it on her mind, as if she were taking a photograph. She wanted to remember this place forever. It would warm the cold nights in Boston when she returned…

She took a small step back, stumbling on a rock. As she tried to right herself, she heard a strange noise behind her. A low rattle that seemed to vibrate through the very earth.

Clara froze. Slowly, she turned around.

An olive-patterned snake was coiled near a rock. And its tail was flickering angrily. It was tense, staring straight at her with its beady eyes.

Oh, sweet Lord, thought Clara, feeling like she was going to faint. *It is a rattlesnake. And I am going to die out here!*

She had no idea what to do. There were no poisonous snakes in Boston, and she had never encountered a snake in her life, regardless. She had been reckless to wander so far. Hannah had warned her. But like the fool she was, she had plundered on, heedless of the dangers that surrounded her.

Just like this entire journey, she thought, her heart flipping over with fear.

"Stay still. Don't move."

Clara gasped, turning her head. It was Jeb atop a horse, his hat pulled down low. She watched him dismount, tying the horse to a tree, before walking towards her. His movements were slow and deliberate.

He drew close to her, taking her arm firmly.

"Walk slowly," he whispered. "One small step at a time. Don't let panic overwhelm you. Sudden movement alarms them, and they strike quickly."

Clara felt sweat trickling down her neck. She swallowed hard, nodding, letting him lead her away from the snake. It seemed to take forever. But eventually, they were out of the snake's range.

Clara burst into tears. "I'm so sorry," she whispered.

Jeb's green eyes were solemn. "You shouldn't stray too far," he said, shaking his head. "You don't know the terrain. We have a *lot* of snakes here, including the black-tailed rattler that you just encountered. But there's also scorpions, spiders, panthers, and coyotes…"

Clara swallowed painfully again. "Oh, I *have* been foolish!" She hesitated. "Thank you, Jeb. If you hadn't arrived in time, I might be dead by now."

He grinned slightly. "I came looking for you when Ma told me you had been gone too long. I'm just glad I found you in time, too." His eyes swept over her. "You're a city girl through and through, Clara, aren't you?"

Clara's face burnt deeply. It sounded like an accusation. But how could she apologize for where she had lived her entire life? Or for who she was?

I do not belong here, she thought mournfully. *I would never survive, even if Jeb changed his mind about wanting a wife. It is best that I am going back to where I came from.*

He placed her on the horse's back before mounting it himself. And then, in the blink of an eye, they were galloping away. Clara clung to his back as the landscape whizzed by. It was the very first time she had ridden a horse, and it was overwhelming but exciting. Especially clinging to the back of the muscular man.

He had protected her. She felt so safe and secure when he was around, as if she never wanted to let him go. And he was kind and clever, too, recalling how he had spoken with her that night on the front porch. She had been wrong about Jeb Huxley. Her first impression of him was not who he was. He was far, far more than that.

He would have made a very good husband. It is my loss.

As they slowed down, approaching the ranch, Clara felt a wave of sorrow sweep over her. If only things had been different. If only he wanted her, as she was starting to want him. But Jeb Huxley didn't want a wife…and he didn't want her. He thought her too much of a delicate city slicker, apart from everything else. The sooner she accepted that fact and left Cloud Springs, the better.

Chapter Seven

That evening at supper, Jeb couldn't stop looking at Clara across the table. She had been so shaken by her encounter with the rattler that day and so sweetly apologetic for wandering too far.

She is such a beautiful, gentle woman, he thought suddenly. *She will make someone a wonderful wife one day.*

He frowned, tearing off a hunk of bread and mopping up the gravy on his plate. She couldn't become his wife, though, no matter how sweet and lovely she was. He didn't want a wife. But besides that, she was hopelessly out of her depth here. Clara had been raised in a city, and she wasn't used to working at all. He needed a strong frontier woman for a wife if he was ever going to take one. A woman who could haul water and chop wood and knew how to deal with snakes and spiders.

His frown deepened. He had been wrong about her. She wasn't arrogant, not really. She was just used to a totally different way of life.

He glanced at her again. This time, she was looking at him, too. Their eyes caught and held for a long moment before he gazed down at his plate again.

His heart shifted. He would be sorry to see her go. But that was life. He couldn't afford to get attached to her, not even a little bit. It would just make it so much harder to say goodbye.

***

The night of the Cloud Springs annual Christmas pageant finally arrived. Clara joined the others in the wagon heading into town, dressed in one of her finest frocks.

"You are so fashionable," said Lillian, sighing heavily as she patted her swollen stomach. "I wish I could wear frocks like that."

Clara smiled at her. "Well, you will be able to once you have had your babe, Lillian. How long before it is due?"

"Mid-January," replied Lillian, sighing again. "Or at least that's what old Doc Lee says. But I think it might be earlier. The babe is carrying so low, and I'm so tired."

Clara reached out, squeezing Lillian's hand. She liked the other girl. Clara had never had a sister, and she was starting to realize how nice it was to become friends with a woman around her age. She and Lillian often sat in the parlor at Cordillera, reading Clara's fashion magazines she had brought with her, exchanging ideas for dresses. She was going to miss the easy companionship.

I am going to miss a lot about Cloud Springs, she thought ruefully, tears springing into her eyes. *But there is no way I can stay here. More is the pity.*

"How pretty you look this evening, Clara," said Hannah, nodding approvingly. "That material in your dress is just lovely." She turned to her son, who had just climbed aboard the wagon, taking the reins. "Don't you think so, Jeb?"

Clara blushed furiously. Jeb glanced at her quickly.

"Mighty pretty," he said in a sarcastic voice, before flicking the reins. The wagon started moving.

Clara turned her face away from the others. She knew he was just being polite. Hannah had put him on the spot. Jeb didn't think she was anything special, even if he did look at her a lot. She knew he felt her totally inappropriate and would be glad to see the back of her. Especially since he had rescued her from the encounter with the rattlesnake.

She didn't know why Jeb Huxley was so adamant he didn't want a wife. But she was sure she had done nothing to change his mind about it. She would be gone in a week, anyway. And Cloud Springs and Cordillera and everyone within it would soon fade to a distant memory.

***

The small church hall was teeming with people when they finally arrived. The Huxleys nodded and smiled at their neighbours as they took seats towards the front.

Clara gazed around in wonder. The hall was decorated so beautifully, with intertwining ivy and holly. A large Christmas tree was alight with candles at the back. It was so magical that Clara felt her breath catch in her throat.

The lights dimmed, and the curtain opened. Clara sat back, watching the nativity play unfold. She smiled as the angels entered, declaring the birth of the Christ child. She had helped make their wings, and they were perfect in their flowing white gowns and wire golden halos. It was such a small achievement, and yet, she had never felt prouder of anything in her life.

This community is wonderful, she thought, holding back tears. *And I feel like I have truly been a part of it, even if it was only for a short while.*

Her mind drifted back to her past Christmases in Boston with Uncle Eustace. The large, cold house that was so beautifully decorated but devoid of life and spirit. The expensive gifts for her under the Christmas tree, so tastefully wrapped, yet purchased by servants. The strained Christmas luncheon, where she and her uncle sat across from each other dining on a feast fit for a king, yet rarely speaking, before going their separate ways.

She realized there had been no Christmas spirit in that house, no matter how grand it was. But here, in this small church hall in the middle of nowhere, it abounded. Most of these people weren't rich. But Clara suddenly realized they were rich in a far more important way.

***

After the pageant ended and they said goodbye to everyone, Hannah insisted that Clara sit next to Jeb at the front of the wagon while she, Lillian, and the children rode in the back, beneath the canopy. Clara felt awkward, but she didn't know how to refuse. And Jeb didn't say anything, either.

As they drove through the sleepy town, Clara gasped. Small lanterns had appeared as if they had sprung from the earth itself, dotting the main street. The lights flickered and bobbed in the darkness, creating a magical, ethereal beauty.

"What are they?" she breathed, enchanted.

Jeb glanced at her. "They are called *luminarias*," he replied, smiling slightly. "They are traditional here at Christmas."

"How are they made?"

"Just brown paper bags weighted down with sand," he said, turning to look at her. "With a candle inside. They don't cost much to make."

"It is so beautiful here," said Clara in a dreamy voice. "And I love the traditions. It is so different to Christmas at home."

They headed out of town, leaving the glowing lanterns behind. Instead, a full moon lit their path, hanging in the sky like an overripe peach on the branch, shimmering and pearlescent. As the wagon traversed the slightly hilly road, Clara felt like they were chasing it.

"There is a local legend about the moon," said Jeb, his voice drifting towards her in the darkness. "Do you want to hear it?"

Clara's heart skipped a beat. "Yes, please."

Jeb nodded, looking pleased. "The old people say the moon is a maiden," he said slowly. "She was the first woman in the world and also the most beautiful. They say that all life springs from her."

Clara smiled. "That is a lovely tale."

Jeb turned to her, watching her face. "But I don't think they are right," he said in an odd voice. "I think they got it wrong. I think *you* might be the most beautiful woman in the world, and the moon can't hold a candle to you."

Clara's heart somersaulted in her chest. She could barely breathe.

He thinks me the most beautiful woman in the world. I feel like I have been given the greatest gift of my life.

The trip was almost over. They turned down the narrow dirt road leading to Cordillera, and Clara's heart swelled. She felt like she never wanted to get off this wagon, like she wanted to ride beside him, chasing the moon into Mexico. Or perhaps to the end of the earth itself.

"You think me beautiful?" she whispered in a halting voice.

"Yes, I do," he said slowly. "You *are* beautiful…but that isn't even the half of it. Your kindness and sweetness are even more luminous than your beauty. You aren't anything like I thought you were when I first met you." He hesitated. "I will be sad to see you go, Clara."

Clara's heart plummeted. She had been so wrong about him in so many ways. And to her utter amazement, he didn't dislike her. His sweet words to her hovered in the air, intangible. She wanted to reach out a hand and grasp them, to never let them go. But already, they were drifting away on the breeze.

Despite those sweet words, he was still willing to let her go. Yes, he would be sad. But he was prepared to do it. And he would forget about her soon enough. In one way, she wished he had never said those words to her at all. It might make the leaving easier to bear.

Chapter Eight

Christmas Eve arrived at Cordillera, with it an almost palpable excitement. Clara watched fondly as Lillian's three children ran around the house, sneaking to the Christmas tree when their mother and grandmother weren't looking to shake the presents beneath, trying to guess what was within.

"I wish Roy could have made it back for Christmas," Lillian sighed, shaking her head. "Lord knows he tried, but he couldn't." She bit her lip, frowning slightly, as she rubbed her back. "I have a little pain today. The babe seems to be pressing on a nerve. It's no wonder. It's as big as a foal!"

Clara laughed. "Will you stay back this evening to rest?"

Lillian shook her head. "Oh, no. The Christmas Eve bonfire is one of the biggest events in Cloud Springs, and so much fun! The children will never forgive me if I don't make the effort. I will soldier on."

It was almost dusk by the time they all climbed aboard the wagon, heading into town. The bonfire was to be held in the only park in town.

Clara gasped when they arrived, taking it all in. There were *luminarias* everywhere, aglow in the semi-darkness, lighting a path to the bonfire in the middle of the park, which crackled and roared, sending sparks into the air like a thousand tiny fireflies. There were even tumbleweeds dressed like snowmen dotted around the park, which made Clara smile. She supposed it was a southwestern tradition to use what the desert provided in the absence of snow!

It looked like simply *everyone* in the town had decided to come. Clara saw Mrs. Vickers with her baby, May, who was swaddled tightly against the cold. Some women were manning stalls, dishing out hot cinnamon churros, fresh empanadas, and cinnamon-spiced hot chocolate, which were part of the Spanish Christmas traditions of the southwest. Most people were crowded around the bonfire, chatting and laughing, warming their hands against the fire.

Clara felt her heart shift. It was the most exquisite, touching spectacle she had ever beheld.

She watched as Jeb melted into the crowd, chatting with his neighbors. She couldn't take her eyes off him as the night progressed. He was clearly well respected in the town—people sought him out to speak to him. But as cordial as he was with them all, Clara noticed he took a lot of time tending to his niece and nephews, even carrying Robbie, the four-year-old, on his shoulders for some of the evening.

He will make a good father one day, thought Clara, feeling a stab of pain. *And he will make someone a fine husband.*

Pearl, Jimmy, and Robbie gathered up at some point to join the Christmas carols.

Clara sat back near the fire, closing her eyes, as "Silent Night," "O Come All Ye Faithful," "Joy to the World," and many others rang out in the night air. A single tear trickled down her cheek as they sang "What Child is this?" for it had always been her favorite Christmas carol. She couldn't help singing out with the last verse.

> *Raise, raise the song on high!*
> *The virgin sings her lullaby,*
> *Joy! Joy! For Christ is born*
> *The babe, the son of Mary*

Clara opened her eyes as the song faded into the night. She yawned discreetly. It was getting so late, and she wouldn't be surprised if the night had already expired and ticked over into Christmas Day. But as tired as she was, she didn't want it to end. She *never* wanted this enchanted night to end. If only she could cling to it forever…

"Clara." It was Jeb, standing in front of her, his voice full of urgency. "We must get back to Cordillera. Lillian's time has come."

Clara paled, standing up quickly. "What? Where is she?"

"Already in the wagon," said Jeb, frowning slightly. "I'm going to speak to the doctor to follow us, then we must leave immediately. Go on."

Clara nodded, pushing through people to get to the wagon. Hannah was assisting Lillian into the back. The younger woman's face was filled with pain, and Clara saw the sweat upon her brow. The children had already been bundled into the back, looking frightened.

As soon as Lillian was safely aboard, Hannah turned to Clara, her eyes dark with worry. "It is too early," she said in a frantic whisper. "Doc Lee said she wasn't due until January! Oh, sweet Lord, I hope and pray my girl will be safe and that her babe will arrive safely."

Clara squeezed the older woman's arm. "I'm sure it will be alright. We must pray."

When Jeb finally returned to the wagon, they set off, hurtling into the night. Clara barely noticed the town or the *luminarias* or anything else. She glanced at Jeb. He was silent, concentrating on the drive, his brow furrowed with worry.

Please, dear Lord, look after Lillian, she prayed, staring at the night sky. *And deliver her baby safely.*

Once back at Cordillera, they rushed inside the house. Hannah took Lillian to a spare room, preparing the bed. The three children hung back, watching as their grandmother assisted their mother into the bed, looking like they were about to burst into tears.

Clara bit her lip. Hannah was preoccupied with Lillian. She must help.

"Come along," she said to them in a firm but gentle voice. "You must get ready for bed. You don't want to sleep in on Christmas morning, do you?"

They followed her willingly. She read book after book to them before they finally fell asleep and she could return to the room. The doctor had arrived. Hannah was bustling around. She looked relieved when she saw Clara.

"Is there anything else you want me to do?" asked Clara.

At that moment, Lillian let out a low moan of pain, clawing at the sheets on the bed. Clara's heart lurched in panic. She had never witnessed childbirth before. Could she handle it?

Of course you can, she told herself sternly. *You cannot turn and run away at hardship. This is a part of life. And you are no longer the pampered, spoilt woman you once were. That life is gone forever.*

"Yes," replied Hannah in a harassed voice. "Boil some water on the stove. And bring more sheets."

Clara nodded quickly. She performed menial chores for the rest of the night as Lillian's labor progressed. Clara had never seen anyone in so much pain, and she wondered how the other woman could endure it. But eventually, hours later, Lillian's babe arrived into the world with a loud, squawking cry.

Clara couldn't help it. Tears streamed down her face as the doctor handed Lillian her newborn child, swaddled in a towel. Lillian was crying, as well. Even capable, resilient Hannah had tears in her eyes.

"It's a girl," whispered Lillian, her eyes shining.

"She is beautiful," said Clara, a lump in her throat the size of a pebble.

Eventually, she stumbled out of the room in a daze, surprised to see the first rays of dawn streaking across the sky as she headed to the front porch for some air. And then she remembered. It was the dawn of Christmas Day. She had never been up so early to greet the holy Day before.

Clara leaned against the porch railing, breathing deeply. She had never been so exhausted and elated in her life. It had been a profound experience witnessing the birth of Lillian's daughter. And that tiny girl shared her birthday with the Christ child, which made her a very special little girl indeed.

"Is there news?"

Clara spun around. Jeb was standing there, dressed in his work gear, his hat upon his head.

"You aren't working on Christmas Day, are you?" she breathed.

"Only for a couple of hours," he said, his moss-green eyes cloudy with exhaustion. "There's some cattle stuck in a stream."

"Have you had any sleep at all?"

He shook his head. "No. But then, it looks like you haven't either." He took a step towards her. "Is it over? Or is Lillian…"

"It's over," said Clara quickly, smiling at him. "Both mother and child are doing well." She took a deep breath. "Lillian delivered a little girl."

A huge grin broke out over Jeb's face. "A girl? Why, that's wonderful!" He shook his head in wonder. "I wish Roy was here. He will be so upset he missed the birth of his new daughter."

Clara nodded. A wave of exhaustion washed over her.

Jeb took another step towards her, taking her arm. "You are overcome. Thank you so much for what you have done for my sister, Clara. You didn't have to do it."

"Of course I did," said Clara in a small voice. "It was the least I could do to repay your family's hospitality. And besides, I am no longer the useless woman I was before I came here. Or at least, I am trying hard not to be."

There was an awkward pause. A wave of emotion seemed to crash between them. Jeb stared at her hard, his green eyes flickering in the early morning light.

"This has been the most wonderful experience of my life," continued Clara, her voice breaking. "I love Cordillera. I love Cloud Springs. And I love your family." She hesitated. "I will be so sorry to say goodbye tomorrow…"

Jeb's hand tightened on her arm. "What do you mean? You can't leave! I won't let you!"

Clara gaped at him. "I must leave. You know that I must. And besides, I already have my ticket on the noon train." She paused, staring at him. "I cannot remain as an unwanted guest in your home any longer…"

Jeb shook his head vigorously. His face was tight with emotion.

"No," he said in an urgent low voice. "You are not unwanted here, Clara Whittaker. You are wanted. Very much." His eyes flickered over her face. "I've been trying to fight it so hard. I thought I couldn't marry yet. I thought you were unsuitable for this life. But I realize now that none of it matters."

Clara gaped at him, so shocked she couldn't speak.

"I love you, Clara," he said, his voice wavering. "*I love you*. I've been such a fool, fighting it, but I've been falling in love with you this whole time. I know we got off to a wrong start. But please…say you will marry me and stay."

Clara gasped, flinging her arms around his neck. She was almost delirious with exhaustion, and it had been the most challenging night of her life, but she had never been happier than she had at this moment. All her dreams were coming true…and in an even better way than she could ever have imagined.

"Yes," she whispered. "Oh, yes, I will marry you, Jeb Huxley! For I love you, too. So very much."

He picked her up, twirling her around. They were both laughing with joy and exhaustion. And when he gently placed her on the ground again, Clara gasped anew, staring at the sky. Tiny snowflakes were drifting down from the sky, dissolving before reaching the ground. Clara's heart flipped. It wasn't a thick covering, but it *was* snow on Christmas Day.

"I told you," whispered Jeb, grinning again. "I told you it sometimes snows here for Christmas…"

Clara laughed with joy, grabbing his hand and dragging him off the porch into the yard. They danced as the tiny snowflakes drifted around them. And Clara knew, without a shadow of a doubt, that it was not only the start of her brand-new life but that this was the most magical Christmas ever.

Epilogue

A month later

Clara took a deep breath as she hovered in the church doorway, straightening her white gown. Her heart lurched with anxiety and shock. The church was packed with people. It looked like the whole town had turned out to witness her marrying Jeb Huxley!

Oh, dear Lord, she thought, feeling like she was about to faint away entirely. *How am I going to do this?*

Her wedding day had finally arrived. The Lord knew it had been a rocky road to get here. She and her intended husband had clashed at the start. Jeb had never even sent for her and hadn't wanted a wife. She had almost been about to leave Cloud Springs forever.

This shouldn't be happening, thought Clara. *And yet, by some miracle, it is.*

"Ready?" asked Doc Lee, who was standing in for her father to walk her down the aisle.

Clara smiled up at the kind, elderly man, dressed in his Sunday best. He had been tickled pink when she had asked him to do this for her, telling her that he would be honored. But he seemed the most appropriate candidate, considering he had delivered Lillian's baby safely. A babe that Clara was godmother to, now.

Her eyes sought out Lillian, in the front pew, holding that precious baby girl. She had been named Holly, for having been born on Christmas Day. Clara knew she would always have a special bond with little Holly. For hadn't she been present when the child had been born?

Sitting next to Lillian were the other children, Hannah, and Lillian's husband Roy, who had finally made it back home after New Year to meet his new daughter. Clara liked

Roy – he was gruff but funny. He loved his wife and family. And Clara loved them all, as well. They were *her* family now. A family she had never believed she would ever have, as well as a whole new life she had never imagined either.

The church organ started blaring the Wedding March. Clara took Doc Lee's arm, walking down the aisle.

And finally, her eyes turned to him. Jeb.

He was waiting patiently at the front, looking nervous in his new suit. His eyes lit up as he watched her drift towards him. Clara gasped as she saw the love in his green eyes. A love that existed solely for her.

They joined hands, facing each other. Clara stared into the eyes of the man who was just about to become her husband. How she loved him. And how she loved the life they were about to create together.

She knew it was not going to be an easy life. But it would be a life filled with joy, as well as hardship. She was sure of it. And maybe, God willing, children of their own.

As the preacher's voice washed over her, Clara knew it had all been worth it: the risk, the sacrifice, the long journey, the uncertainty. She wouldn't change a thing about it. Not at all.

The End

FREE GIFT

Just to say thanks for checking our works we like to gift you

Our Exclusive Never Before Released Books

100% FREE!

Please GO TO

`http://cleanromancepublishing.com/gift`

And get your FREE gift

Thanks for being such a wonderful client.

Please Check out My Other Works

By checking out the link below

http://cleanromancepublishing.com/fjauth

Thank You

Many thanks for taking the time to buy and read through this book.

It means lots to be supported by SPECIAL readers like YOU.

Hope you enjoyed the book; please support my writing by leaving an honest review to assist other readers.

.

With Regards,

Faith Johnson

Printed in Great Britain
by Amazon

36470831R00058